To My Mother Hen and Dad
J.L.

Copyright © 2013 by NordSüd Verlag AG, CH-8005 Zürich, Switzerland.
First published in Switzerland under the title *Mama Huhns großer Tag*.
English translation copyright © 2013 by NorthSouth Books Inc., New York 10016.
Translated by Rebecca K. Morrison.

First published in the United States, Great Britain, Canada, Australia, and New Zealand in 2013
by NorthSouth Books Inc., an imprint of NordSüd Verlag AG, CH-8005 Zürich, Switzerland.

Distributed in the United States by NorthSouth Books Inc., New York 10016.
Library of Congress Cataloging-in-Publication Data is available.
Printed in Germany by Grafisches Centrum Cuno GmbH & Co. KG, Calbe, Germany
in November 2012.

FSC
www.fsc.org
MIX
Paper from
responsible sources
FSC® C043106

ISBN: 978-0-7358-4109-3
1 3 5 7 9 · 10 8 6 4 2
www.northsouth.com

Mama Hen's Big Day!

by Jill Latter

This is Mama Hen.
Today is an important day for her.

Today she is going to lay an egg. But first she has to find the right place—the loveliest, safest, most peaceful place of all.

Only the best will do for Mama Hen's egg.

Mama Hen hurries on her way.

The cave looks cozy. But somebody else thinks so too.

The meadow looks peaceful.
But who is that?

It's the neighbor's cat—
lying in wait. Quick,
head for the hills!

The leaves look lovely. But watch your step!

A porcupine has already curled up and made himself a home. Keep going, Mama Hen!

The tall grass seems safe. But who is hiding?

It's a little red fox.

Mama Hen is getting worried.
Where, oh, where is the best place
for a hen to lay her egg?

Round and round and higher and higher Mama Hen goes. Where is the best place for her egg?

At last, Mama Hen reaches the tippy-top
of the tallest mountain . . .

and lays her egg.

For, on this important
day, Mama Hen has
made a discovery. . . .
The best place of all
to lay her egg is
wherever Mama is!